A BAG FULL OF

NOTHING

written by JAY WILLIAMS

illustrated by TOM O'SULLIVAN

Parents' Magazine Press / *New York*

OTHER BOOKS BY JAY WILLIAMS

The Cookie Tree
Forgetful Fred
The King With Six Friends
Petronella
The Practical Princess
A Present From A Bird
School For Sillies
Seven At One Blow
The Silver Whistle
Stupid Marco
The Youngest Captain

For my grandson Jesse with a bag full of love

Tip and his father were leaning on the
railing of the bridge, looking at the stream.
Mr. Wellcome had just finished telling Tip
a story about a magic ring, a prince,
a princess, and three wishes.

Tip sighed, watching the smooth brown
water. There were bubbles along its edge
as big as tea cups.

"Is there really magic?" he asked.

"I don't know, Tip. Lots of things seem
like magic."

"I think there is magic," said Tip, making
up his mind.

Tip and his father began walking home.
Suddenly Tip stopped. In the middle of the
road was a neatly folded brown paper bag.
"Where did that come from?" he asked.
"Someone must have dropped it," said
Mr. Wellcome.

Tip looked up at the sky. "A big, strange bird," he said, imagining. "I think it's a magic bag."
He picked it up.
He opened it and looked inside. "It's full of magic."
"No, Tip," said his father. "I don't think so. It's a bag full of nothing."
"You'll see," Tip said.

He walked on, carrying the paper bag.
A little further on they came to a place where,
beside the road, blackberries were growing in a
tangle of prickly bushes.

Mr. Wellcome plucked a berry and tasted it.
"Yum!" he said. "They're just right."
He and Tip began to pick blackberries. Soon,
Mr. Wellcome had a handful. That was all he
could hold. But Tip went right on picking.
He was putting berries in the paper bag.
"I think I have a lot more than you, Pa,"
he said. "Now you see—it's not a bag full of
nothing, it's a bag full of berries."
"Hm," said his father, and that was all he said.

They walked on together, eating berries. When
Mr. Wellcome's berries were all gone, Tip gave
him some from the bag. When the bag was
empty Mr. Wellcome said, "Now it's a bag full
of nothing again."

"No, it isn't," insisted Tip. "You'll see."

They came to a crossroad. People were waiting
at the bus stop.

"Yikes!" said Tip. "There's Mrs. Goodyear."

Mrs. Goodyear was a nice fat old lady who had one bad habit. Every time she talked to a child, she pinched. She pinched cheeks, cooing, "And how are we today?" She pinched ears, asking,

"And have we been a good little boy—or a good
little girl—today?"

"I don't want to be pinched," Tip said.
"Let's run."

"We can't do that. She's seen us," replied
his father.

Tip opened the paper bag. He put it over
his head.

"Hello, Mrs. Goodyear," said Tip's father.

"Hello, Mr. Wellcome," Mrs. Goodyear chirped.
She looked at the bag in surprise. There was
nothing to pinch. "Well," she said. "Well,
how are we today?"

"We're fine," said Mr. Wellcome. "In a hurry.
Good-bye."

He grabbed Tip's hand and led him away.

Tip muttered something inside the bag.

"What?" said his father.

"It's not a bag full of nothing, it's a bag full of head."

"Oh," said his father.

"Is she there?"

"Not anymore."

Tip pulled off the bag.

"Now it's a bag full of nothing again,"
laughed his father.

"No, it isn't," Tip said sternly. "You'll see."

Just outside the village, they came to a big gray
house. A man named Mr. Huff lived there.
He had a small, fierce, bad-tempered dog.
As Tip and his father neared the house, they heard
the dog barking.

"Don't be afraid," said Mr. Wellcome. "Just stand still for a minute."

The dog came bounding across the lawn, making
a furious racket.

Tip blew the bag up full of air. He held the
top tightly closed. Then he hit the bag as hard
as he could.

BANG!

The dog skidded to a stop. He turned smack
around and almost fell flat. Away he ran with his
tail between his legs.

"There," said Tip. "It was a bag full of noise!"

Mr. Wellcome scratched his head. "I guess you
were right," he said. "It was a kind of magic
bag after all."

Tip opened it and looked inside. "Now it's got
a hole in it," he said sadly.

"A bag full of holes?"

"No, just one hole. But that's enough. There's
no more bag."

"Well," said his father, putting a hand on Tip's shoulder. "In fairytales there are always three wishes, or three marvelous adventures. That's what you had, so that makes it even more magical."

Tip looked worried. "And now I guess I'll have to marry the princess and live happily ever after."

"Not just yet," said his father. "But you can have an ice cream cone and live happily ever after until dinner."

Jay Williams is the author of more than fifty books—fiction as well as non-fiction—for both children and adults, including the popular *Danny Dunn* science fiction series. Mr. Williams' twelve books for Parents' Magazine Press include *The Silver Whistle,* selected as one of the Fifty Best Books of the Year by the American Institute of Graphic Arts, and *The Practical Princess,* winner of a Golden Apple Award at the Biennale of Illustrations at Bratislava, Czechoslovakia.

Tom O'Sullivan, a veteran free-lance illustrator, has illustrated many children's books. Mr. O'Sullivan taught drawing and composition at the School of Visual Arts in New York City, and is the recipient of the Society of Illustrators Medal. He lives in New York with his wife and daughter, travels extensively, keeps sketchbooks of his travel experiences, and summers in Martha's Vineyard where he sails his own sloop.